I Am Brave

A
**POSITIVE
POWER**
STORY

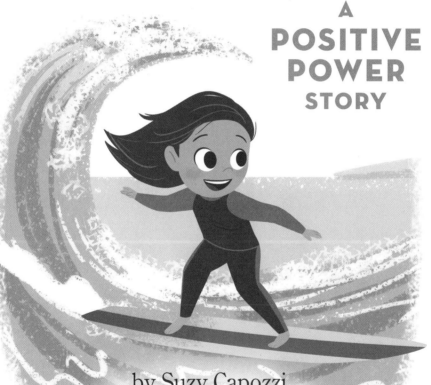

by Suzy Capozzi
illustrated by Eren Unten

Random House 🏠 New York

We are going on a trip.
It is my first time on a plane.
I am a little nervous.
So I try to read a book.

Tim calls me **Scaredy Kat**.
Mom tells Tim to buckle up
and behave.

I close my eyes.
The plane takes off.

It feels like a roller coaster.

I like roller coasters.

I'm not scared anymore. I am brave.

We unpack at the hotel.

Then we go to the pool.

Tim and I head for the waterslide.

At the top, we get in a tube.

It looks like a **wild** river below.

But Tim leads the way, and I let go.

We splash and laugh
the whole way down.
We are brave.

The next day, we go horseback riding.
My horse's name is Big Ben.
How will I get up there?
Will I fall off his back?

A teacher shows me the ropes.
I trust Big Ben and he trusts me.

Later, we ride on the beach.
Big Ben and I make a good team.
I am brave.

Another day, we hike
in the woods.
We see birds and lizards.

We climb down to a spooky cave.
Mom won't go in.
Maybe I will stay with her.

I decide to go inside.
It is dark and cool.
There are tiny holes in the
top of the cave.

They look like stars.
We see some bats, too.
They don't scare me.
I am brave.

It is the last day of our trip.
Mom says the waves are
perfect for surfing.

First, we practice on the beach.

In the water, Mom shows us how to stand up.

Dad shows us how to belly flop.

We paddle out.
A big wave comes in.
I take a deep breath
and exhale slowly.

I can do this.
I jump up on my board.

I catch the wave!
I am brave.

That night, we go to a party.
I see food I have never tried.

I try it. It's yummy!
After we eat, everyone dances.

There is a magic show, too.
The magician needs help.
We all raise our hands.

He picks me!

I put on a cape and get into the big box.
It is very dark inside, but I'm not afraid.

The magician waves his wand.

He opens the box. It is empty.
Everyone gasps.

Ta-da!
I'm back!

Tim wants to know the magician's secret.
I'll never tell.
He gives me a **new** nickname—
Kat the Brave.
Tim is right.
I am brave!

For Cheryl, the brave

—S.C.

To Dad, with love

—E.U.

Text copyright © 2018 by Suzy Capozzi
Cover art and interior illustrations copyright © 2018 by Eren Unten

All rights reserved. Published in the United States by Random House Children's Books, a division of Penguin Random House LLC, New York. Originally published by Rodale Kids, an imprint of Random House Children's Books, a division of Penguin Random House LLC, New York, in 2018.

Step into Reading, Random House, and the Random House colophon are registered trademarks of Penguin Random House LLC.

Visit us on the Web!
StepIntoReading.com
rhcbooks.com

Educators and librarians, for a variety of teaching tools, visit us at
RHTeachersLibrarians.com

Library of Congress Cataloging-in-Publication Data is available upon request.
ISBN 978-0-593-43415-4 (trade) — ISBN 978-0-593-43414-7 (lib. bdg.) —
ISBN 978-0-593-43416-1 (ebook)

Printed in the United States of America
10 9 8 7 6 5 4 3 2 1

This book has been officially leveled by using the F&P Text Level Gradient™ Leveling System.